PIG the ELF

Dear Santa,

May I please have
something nice
for Christmas?

        from Trevor

PS-I love you so much!

For Andrew, Ana, Beck, and Nicole —
You're just the best.

ISBN 978-1-338-23004-8
10 9 8 7 6 5 4 3 2 1   17 18 19 20 21

Printed in the U.S.A.   08
First printing 2017

The artwork in this book is acrylic (with pens and pencils) on watercolor paper.
The type was set in Adobe Caslon.

PIG the ELF

Aaron Blabey

Scholastic Inc.

Oh, Christmas Eve!
That most merry of nights!
The carols! The snowflakes!
The small, twinkly lights!

Santa was coming!
'Twas bigger than big,
but no one was feeling
more festive than . . .

for PIG

PIG!

How he loved Christmas!
He'd giggle with glee —
"The presents! The presents!
For ME! ME! ME! ME!"

He'd written his list,
and he'd asked for a lot.
But Santa takes orders,
so why the heck not?

I WANT:
A MOTORCYCLE
A ROCKET
A DRUM SET
A PONY
A SKATEBOARD
A COTTON CANDY
MAKER
A TRA

Dear Santa,

May I please have
something nice
for Christmas?

from Trevor

PS-I love yo

"The presents! THE PRESENTS!!"
He screamed out again.
"*When* will he get here?
Oh, WHEN?
TELL ME WHEN?!"

"He'll come when we sleep,"
said his lovely friend, Trevor.

But Pig shouted,

"SLEEP?
I'll have none
whatsoever!"

"Sleep is for fools!
Oh yes, sleep is for losers!
I won't go to bed
with the rest of you snoozers!

I'm sitting up late!
I'll be here when he comes!
I declare by these stockings
and gingerbread crumbs!"

for Santa

So Trevor went dutifully
off to his bed.

But naughty old Pig
stayed up, just like he said.

The waiting was endless,
but Pig held his ground.
Then at three thirty-three,
well, he heard a strange sound . . .

And guess who had made
that mysterious noise?
A portly old gent . . .
with a bag full of toys!

He piled up some presents
marked "Trevor" and "Pig,"
then he picked up his milk
and he took a big swig.

But then, as he turned
to go back on his way,

Trevor

Pig

a short cranky dog appeared,
shouting out,

"HEY!"

"I asked for MORE!"
hollered Pig in dismay.
But Santa turned 'round
and then hurried away.

"Hey!" shouted Pig,
sounding very unkind.

Then he nipped poor old Santa's big, rosy behind!

Up through the chimney . . .

Out to the sleigh . . .

Pig held on tight.
"You're not getting away!
Don't be a cheapskate!
I want all my stuff!
The pile that you left me

IS JUST NOT ENOUGH!"

But the sleigh took off fast.

Gee, those reindeer were speedy!

And away fell their guest —

Yes, the elf who was greedy.

But as Trevor lay dreaming
of holiday cheer,
a real Christmas miracle
happened right here . . .

Yes, Pig must be blessed.
He survived that big drop,
and was saved by a tree . . .

. . . with an angel on top.

I WANT:

A MOTORCYCLE

A ROCKET

A DRUM SET

A PONY

A SKATEBOARD

A COTTON CANDY MAKER

A TRAINED SHARK

A BAG OF FUDGE

ANOTHER

A CAPE

A JETSKI

AN INFLATABLE BANANA

TRIP TO A MAJOR THEME PARK

THREE SKATEBOARDS ACTUALLY

SCUBA GEAR

FALSE TEETH

A CHARIOT

ROLLERBLADES

A UNICORN (REAL, NOT FAKE)

STIL

A NUR

UNIF

A CAN

A P

JAC

A WAT

MAK

Fo

SKAT

LON
BE

AN

'S
M
N
Y
T

BED

HAT

ARDS

TIFUL

HAIR

SHAKE

ER

ET

WOULD

ONE OF THOSE
HATS WITH A
PROPELLER
ON TOP

A PRETTY
TEA SET

FAKE POO
(FUNNY)

A CAT TO DO
THINGS WITH

BEARD

A LITTLE
ISLAND
(OR A BIG ONE,
DON'T MIND)

40 GALLONS

A BAGPIPER

A CHAINSAW

THE POWER
OF
INVISIBILITY

AS MUCH FRIED
CHICKEN AS
I CAN EAT

12 HULA HOOPS
(MUST BE 12)

A DAY SPA
VOUCHER

FIGURE-SKATING
LESSONS

LONGER LEGS